F

Food For Thought

To,
Smt. SAVITHRI DEVI
WITH EVER
BEST WISHES
— Sityavarayan
18-01-13

Dr M Rajaram

RUPA

This book is dedicated to the youth,
who will turn these pages
and influence the future

Attitude

An optimist sees the difficulty in every opportunity. An optimist sees the opportunity in every difficulty.

When it rains, all the birds fly to shelter. Only the eagle avoids the rain by flying above the clouds. The problem is common to all but attitude makes the difference.

Attitude is like the smell of a letter, it tells the force of its walls, the mood of the reader, even a trip into the mind.

Watch everyway too... thinking about your success. Always maintain an attitude to success... bless free.

Contents

Justice K Venkatasamy
Former Judge
Supreme Court of India

Foreword

Food For Thought by Dr M Rajaram, IAS, is a collection of inspiring words of great men. All the quotations in this book are simple, sincere and therefore effective. Many are expressed brilliantly, dazzling us with their beauty and thoughtfulness. The quotations cover different aspects of life and encompass a very wide range of topics. A few proverbs are also included in the book.

Many schools and colleges display quotations on the noticeboard as a part of their daily routine and hence for such institutions, this can be a very useful sourcebook. The sum of these quotations is a wonderful storehouse where a reader can enter for guidance, amusement or for the sheer joy of being in the company of extraordinary minds.

I derived great pleasure from reading this book. It has an eternal charm and universal appeal.

I commend Dr M Rajaram, IAS, for his scholarly efforts, and I strongly believe the readers of this book will be immensely inspired.

Justice K Venkatasamy

Author's Note

Dr APJ Abdul Kalam says, 'Life without challenges is like food without salt; we cannot enjoy it.'

Today's youth face a lot of challenges. They need emotional support through the inspiring words of eminent personalities.

To inspire self-confidence and hope, this book, *Food For Thought*, containing quotes of moral and emotional values, has been compiled.

This book contains a fair, representative and assorted collection of quotes and sayings on a wide range of topics sourced from various nationalities and cultures, arranged in alphabetical order for ready reference.

Acknowledgements

I gratefully acknowledge the enthusiastic support of my friends and well-wishers – Mr Kapish Mehra, Mr Swaran Singh, IAS, Mr D Varadarajan, Mr CS Kalyanasundaram, Mr P Jeyaraj, Mr C Jeyakrishnan, Dr V Thanigs, Mr DJ Bethelraj, Mr SK Nazer, Dr Agnes Mary, Dr Kavidasan, Mr S Velliyangiri, Prof J Ranganathan, Dr Sivaraman, Mr J Narayanasamy, Mr Rameshsharma, Dr CMK, Dr V Narayanasamy, Mr P Kannan, Mr S Justin Jose, Mr A Poovaraga Moorthy and Mr C Shanmugasundaram.

Achievement

If you are born with fame, it is an accident. If you die with fame, it is your achievement.

— Dr APJ Abdul Kalam

~

Achievers never expose themselves, but their achievements do.

— Anon.

~

If my mind can conceive it and my heart can believe it, I know I can achieve it.

— Jesse Jackson

~

Thinking about yourself is not an achievement. To make others think about you is true achievement.

— Anon.

~

Every new idea is a joke, until one man achieves it.

— Jaggi Vasudev

~

Achievement is largely the product of steadily raising one's level of aspiration and expectation.

— *Jack Nicklaus*

~

To achieve great things, two things are needed: a good plan and not quite enough time.

— *Leonard Bernstein*

~

Little strokes fell great oaks.

— *Benjamin Franklin*

~

Failures are finger posts on the road to achievement.

— *CS Lewis*

~

Definiteness of purpose is the starting point of all achievement.

— *W Clement Stone*

~

Aim

Both 'dream' and 'aim' are sensational words. Make your dream your aim. But, don't make your aim your dream. So, aim high and dream to catch your aim.

— Dr APJ Abdul Kalam

~

An artist was asked at an award function:

'Which is your best painting?'
He replied, 'My next painting.'

Let your future aim be better.

—Jeyakrishnan

~

There is only one difference between dream and aim – dream requires effortless sleep, whereas aim requires sleepless efforts.

— Anon.

~

Anger

The result of anger is more painful than the reason of anger.

— MK Gandhi

~

Care should be in the heart and not in words. Anger should be in words and not in the heart.

— Anon.

~

Whatever is begun in anger ends in shame.

— Benjamin Franklin

~

Holding on to anger is like grasping a hot coal with the intent of throwing it at someone else; you are the one who gets burned.

— Gautama Buddha

~

He who angers you conquers you.

— Elizabeth Kenny

~

Attitude

A pessimist sees the difficulty in every opportunity; an optimist sees the opportunity in every difficulty.

— Anon.

~

When it rains, all the birds occupy shelter. Only the eagle avoids the rain by flying above the clouds. The problem is common to all but attitude makes the difference.

— Osho

~

Advice is like snow; the softer it falls, the longer it dwells upon, and the deeper it sinks into the mind.

— Samuel Taylor Coleridge

~

Whenever you are criticised, don't get upset. Always remember, no stones are thrown at a fruitless tree.

— Anon.

~

Positive attitude creates more miracles than anything else because life is 10% how you make it and 90% how you take it.

— Anon.

~

A person with a positive attitude is like a fruit of all seasons.

— Shiv Khera

~

There is nothing either good or bad, but thinking makes it so.

— William Shakespeare

~

You cannot control what happens to you, but you can control your attitude toward what happens to you, and in that, you will be mastering change rather than allowing it to master you.

— Brian Tracy

~

Your attitude, not your aptitude, will determine your altitude.

— Zig Ziglar

~

Edison failed 10, 000 times before he made the electric light. Do not be discouraged if you fail a few times.

— Napoleon Hill

~

Belief

Your dreams won't die, your plans won't fail, your destiny won't be aborted. The desire of your heart will be granted, only if you believe in yourself!

— Dr APJ Abdul Kalam

~

No one can predict to what heights one can soar. Even you will not know until you spread your wings.

— Dr APJ Abdul Kalam

~

Believe and act as if it were impossible to fail.

— Charles F Kettering

~

A bird sitting on the branch of a tree won't be afraid if the branch is shaken, because the bird trusts its wings more than the branch!

— Anon.

~

Believing everybody is dangerous. Believing nobody is more dangerous.

— *Abraham Lincoln*

~

Believe where others doubt, work where others refuse, save where others waste and stay where others quit. Be different! Believe in yourself!

— *Anon.*

~

To move ahead in your life, you need to believe in yourself, have conviction in your beliefs and the confidence to execute those beliefs.

— *Adlin Sinclair*

~

For those who believe, no proof is necessary. For those who don't believe, no proof is possible.

— *Stuart Chase*

~

All winners do not have to be hard workers! But, surely one day, every hard worker will become a winner. Always do your best.

— *Anon.*

~

The weak believe in luck. The strong believe in hard work.

— *Lewis Carroll*

~

Capacity

Capability is the ability to do better what you are doing. Capacity is doing more of what you are doing.

— Anon.

~

Men are often capable of greater things than they perform. They are sent into the world with bills of credit, and seldom draw to their full extent.

— Sir Hugh Walpole

~

Capacity is the way you respond to adverse situations.

— Anon.

~

As is our confidence, so is our capacity.

— William Hazlitt

~

Everything comes to us that belongs to us if we create the capacity to receive it.

— Rabindranath Tagore

~

Character

The difference between ability and character is that ability will get us to the top but character will retain us at the top.

— Dr APJ Abdul Kalam

~

Thoughts lead on to purposes; purposes go forth in action; actions form habits; habits decide character; and character fixes our destiny.

— Tryon Edwards

~

Men of genius are admired; men of wealth are envied; men of power are feared; but only men of character are trusted.

— Alfred Adler

~

The depth of your character will be revealed in the way you respond to situations you dislike.

— Anon.

~

Always have a unique character, like salt. Its presence is not felt, but its absence is felt.

— Anon.

~

No treasure equals charity. No gem equals character.

— Panchatantra

~

Speak in public only about the good qualities of your friends. But speak nothing about your enemies.

— Adhi

~

Praise loudly; blame softly.

— Catherine the Great

~

If wealth is lost, nothing is lost;
if health is lost, something is lost;
if character is lost, everything is lost.

— Anon.

~

Confidence

Confidence comes naturally with success. But, success comes only to those who are confident.

— Anon.

~

I am not handsome, but I can give my hand to someone.

— Anon.

~

A mirror never loses its ability to reflect even if it is broken into a thousand pieces. Never lose your confidence even when tested a thousand times.

— Anon.

~

Success is like a train. It has several coaches – hard work, focus, luck, etc. But, leading all of them is the engine of confidence.

— Anon.

~

One should walk through the world like the girl carrying five water pots on her head never losing her balance.

— Anon.

~

Men of confidence easily surmount all difficulties.

— Anon.

~

It is not the mountain we conquer, but ourselves.

— Sir Edmund Hillary

~

They can conquer who believe they can.

— Virgil

~

The three great essentials to achieve anything worthwhile are first, hard work; second, stick-to-it-iveness; third, common sense.

— Thomas Alva Edison

~

A good plan for today is better than a great plan for tomorrow. Look backward with satisfaction and look forward with confidence.

— Anon.

~

Act as if it were impossible to fail.

— Dorothea Brande

~

Deeds

Words are mere bubbles of water. Deeds are drops of gold.

— A Chinese proverb

~

There is no better deed than working for others' benefit and there is no greater sin than causing pain to others.

— Anon.

~

A man is great by deeds, not by birth.

— Chanakya

~

Good actions ennoble us, we are the sons of our own deeds.

— Miguel de Cervantes

~

Desire

If you greatly desire something, have the guts to stake everything for achieving it.

— Brendan Francis

~

Curb desires and attain bliss.

— Anon.

~

It is easier to suppress fire than desire.

— Anon.

~

A creative man is motivated by the desire to achieve, not by the desire to beat others.

— Ayn Rand

~

Do not impose on others what you yourself do not desire.

— Confucius

~

Destiny

A race horse knows not why it is running. The pain of being beaten up by its rider impels it to run. Similarly we run the race of life. We are pained by circumstances. It is only through such miseries that god wants us to win.

— Jeyakrishnan

~

Our sweetest songs are those which tell of the saddest thoughts.

— Percy Bysshe Shelly

~

Destiny is not a matter of chance, it is matter of choice.

— William Jennings Bryan

~

Every man meets his waterloo at last.

— Anon.

~

Determination

Be your child's advocate and never assume he or she is wrong.

— Dr APJ Abdul Kalam

~

Determination is the strength you achieve after failure.

— Burkey

~

Victory never fails men of determination.

— Henri Bergson

~

Defeat is not final. It is final only when you refuse to rise up. Always rise up and crush the defeat.

— Anon.

~

Discretion

If the whole world is against you, what'll you do? Simple, just turn your direction, you'll see yourself leading the entire world.

— Napolean Bonaparte

~

Success and excuses do not talk to each other. If you give excuses, forget about success and if you want success, forget about excuses.

— Anon.

~

Discretion is the better part of valour.

— Anon.

~

Sometimes the best gain is to lose.

— George Herbert

~

Discrimination

'No' and 'Yes' are short words which need long thought. Most of the troubles in life are the result of saying 'No' too soon or 'Yes' too late.

— Anon.

~

Popular people are not always genuine. Genuine people are not always popular.

— Charlie Chaplin

~

Make sure the prize you chase is worth the effort.

— Jeyakrishnan

~

The five essential entrepreneurial skills for success are concentration, discrimination, organisation, innovation and communication.

— Michael Faraday

~

Dreams

Every morning you have two choices: either continue dreaming in your sleep or wake up to chase your dreams.

— Anon.

~

Behind all improvements in the world, there have been someone's dreams.

— Justice K Venkatasamy

~

If you can imagine it, you can achieve it. If you can dream it, you can become it.

— William Arthur Ward

~

The dreams of today will be the deeds of tomorrow.

— Anon.

~

Education

Education is not merely a learning process, but it is necessarily a process of transforming humans into better and more efficient individuals.

— Dr APJ Abdul Kalam

~

We must provide excellent facilities for meritorious students; otherwise we will be putting the clock back.

— Dr APJ Abdul Kalam

~

Education makes a people easy to lead, but difficult to drive; easy to govern but impossible to enslave.

— Henry Brougham

~

Destiny of the nation is shaped within the four walls of the classroom.

— Anon.

~

Education is an ornament in prosperity and refuge in adversity.

— Aristotle

~

The merchant's success depends upon the sale of the product; the inspector's success depends on the quality of thoughts which he is able to promote in the minds of headmasters and teachers.

— The Author

~

Teaching ends with the classroom. But education ends only with life.

— Robertson

~

Even the best curriculum and the most perfect syllabus remain dead unless quickened into life by the right methods of teaching and the right kind of teacher.

— Secondary Education Commission

~

Education is the backbone of a progressing nation and the teacher is the pivot in any system of education.

— Dr S Radhakrishnan

~

Schools are the nurseries of the nation. Parents, teachers, headmasters and inspectors are custodians of these nurseries.

— The Author

~

Education is what survives when what has been taught has been forgotten.

— *The Author*

~

The aim of education is the knowledge, not of facts, but of values.

— *William S Burroughs*

~

The three most important priorities of the government are education, education and education.

— *Anon.*

~

The twin objectives of education are intelligence and goodness.

— *The Author*

~

If you educate a man, you educate an individual; but if you educate a woman, you educate a nation.

— *MK Gandhi*

~

Education commences at the mother's lap.

— *Anon.*

~

Literary education is of no value, if it is not able to build up a sound character.

— *MK Gandhi*

~

True education is training of both the head and the heart.

— Anon.

~

Learning is the true imperishable wealth; other things are not wealth.

— Thirukkural

~

Only the educated have the real eyes. The others have sores on their face.

— Thirukkural

~

Magnificent buildings and equipment are no substitutes for great teachers.

— Dr S Radhakrishnan

~

Learning is a process that starts at the time of birth and remains incomplete at the time of death.

— SK Nazer

~

Seven social sins: politics without principles, wealth without work, pleasure without conscience, knowledge without character, commerce without morality, science without humanity, and worship without sacrifice.

— MK Gandhi

~

Enterprise

Thinking is the capital; enterprise is the way; hard work is the solution.

— Anon.

~

'Impossible' doesn't mean that it is not possible. It actually means that nobody has done it so far. You are born to break the limits!

— Rajiv Gandhi

~

If you want something which you never had before, do something which you have never done before.

— Anon.

~

Make the best use of the opportunities god gives you. Whatever you do, do it with all your might, because the door that is open today may not be open tomorrow.

— Anon.

~

We will either find a way, or make one.

— Hannibal

~

Experience

Never reject anybody in your life, because a good person gives us happiness and a bad person gives us experience.

— Anon.

~

Mistakes are painful when they happen, but years later a collection of mistakes is what is called experience.

— Denis Waitley

~

Every experience brings out something good. Good times become good memories, bad times become good lessons. We never lose, we only gain from life.

— Jeyakrishnan

~

If one can do it, you too can do it. If none can do it, you must do it.

— A Japanese proverb

~

Good decisions come from experience. But experience comes from bad decisions.

— Anon.

~

Experience is simply the name we give our mistakes.

— Oscar Wilde

~

Whenever there is a hard job to be done, I assign it to a lazy man; he is sure to find an easy way of doing it.

— Walter Chrysler

~

Experience is the best teacher.

— Anon.

~

If a man deceives me once, shame on him. If he deceives me twice, shame on me.

— Anon.

~

Knowledge comes from experience and experience comes from foolishness.

— Anon.

~

Enthusiasm

A salesman minus enthusiasm is just a clerk.

— Harry F Banks

~

Enthusiasm is the energy and force that builds literal momentum of the human soul and mind.

— Bryant H McGill

~

Nobody grows old merely by living a number of years. We grow old by deserting our ideals. Years may wrinkle the skin, but to give up enthusiasm wrinkles the soul.

— Samuel Ullman

~

Nothing great was ever achieved without enthusiasm.

— Ralph Waldo Emerson

~

The real secret of success is enthusiasm.

— Walter Chrysler

~

Faith

Never lose faith in yourself; you can do anything in this universe. Awake, arise, and stop not till the goal is reached.

— *Swami Vivekananda*

~

What lies behind us and what lies before us are tiny matters compared to what lies within us.

— *Ralph Waldo Emerson*

~

Never seek to please men, for if you please men, you cannot be the servant of god. God has given you this chance to serve Him.

— *DJ Bethelraj*

~

Faith and prayer are the vitamins of the soul; man cannot live in health without them.

— *Mahalia Jackson*

~

Forbearance

If someone hurts you, don't mind, because it is the law of nature that the tree that bears the sweetest fruits gets the maximum number of stones.

— Anon.

~

Forbearance is the best religion.

— Anon.

~

Temper takes you to trouble. Pride keeps you there.

— Anon.

~

Forbearance is the root of quietness and assurance forever.

— Ieyasu Tokugawa

~

Friendship

Nice friends are gifts not easily gained.

— Anon.

~

Friendship roots from the heart where memories stay, not for a moment, not for a day, but forever.

— Anon.

~

Caring friends are the real assets of your life for there is nothing greater than earning good friends.

— SK Nazer

~

A person who searches for friends without faults will never have a friend.

— Anon.

~

Knowingly or unknowingly different people walk into your life but ultimately it's you who decide who stay in and who walk out.

— Anon.

~

The world's happiest friends never have the same characters.
They just have the best understanding of their differences.

— Anon.

~

Never choose a friend without understanding and never lose
a friend because of misunderstanding.

— Anon.

~

When you rise high in life, your friends know who you are!
When you fall down, you know who your friends are.

— Jeyakrishnan

~

Friends are angels who lift our feet when our own wings have
trouble remembering how to fly.

— Anon.

~

Making a million friends is not a miracle. The miracle is
to make a friend who will stand by you when millions are
against you.

— Anon.

~

If friendship is your weakest point, then you are the strongest
person in the world.

— Abraham Lincoln

~

Future

Future is not what we discover tomorrow. But it is the result of what we do today! Do the best in the present.

— Dr APJ Abdul Kalam

~

When your involvement is deeper than the sea and your ambition is taller than a mountain, then your future will be brighter than the sun.

— Anon.

~

Do you know why the windshield is large and the rear-view mirror is small in a car? Because your past is not as important as your future. So look ahead and move on.

— Anon.

~

If you learn to translate every event of your life into a positive one, you are not a prisoner of your past but the designer of your future.

— Anon.

~

The past can't see you, but the future is listening.

— Terri Guillemets

~

The future is not something we should await; it is something we should create.

— Anon.

~

A well-disciplined child today will be a dutiful citizen tomorrow.

— Anon.

~

I do not want to foresee the future. I am concerned with taking care of the present. God has given me no control over the moment following.

— MK Gandhi

~

Change is the law of life. And those who look only to the past or present are certain to miss the future.

— John F Kennedy

~

Giving Up

Giving up doesn't always mean you are weak. Sometimes, it means that you are strong enough to let go.

— Anon.

~

In bad luck, hold out. In good luck, hold in.

— Anon.

~

Winners never quit and quitters never win.

— Anon.

~

It does not matter how slowly you go so long as you do not stop.

— Confucius

~

Never consider the possibility of failure; as long as you persist, you will be successful.

— Brian Tracy

~

God's Grace

God's grace keeps pace with what we face.

— Anon.

~

God can't be everywhere and therefore He made mothers.

— A Jewish proverb

~

You are a precious diamond in god's hands. When god sharpens your edges, it is really painful. But that will only end up making you shine.

— Jeyakrishnan

~

God said 'Build a better world'. I said, 'How? The world is such a complicated, cold dark place and there is nothing I can do'. God said 'Just build a better you'.

— Anon.

~

God is like a software programmer. He 'enters' our life, 'scans' our problems, 'edits' our tension, 'downloads' solutions, 'deletes' our worries and 'saves' us.

— Anon.

~

Golden Words

Always be the reason for someone's happiness and never be just a part of it. Be a part of someone's sadness but never be the reason for it.

— Anon.

~

If you focus on the goal, you overcome all obstacles. If you focus on obstacles, you will never reach your goal.

— Dr APJ Abdul Kalam

~

Never restrict your child's choices. Let your child choose the activity that interests him or her.

— Dr APJ Abdul Kalam

~

Never change your originality for the sake of others because no one can play your role better than you. So be yourself.

— Anon.

~

You need not be great to start with, but you need to start to become great.

— Anon.

~

Those who are most slow in making a promise are the most faithful in the performance of it.

— Jean Jacques Rousseau

~

Know more than the other. Work more than the other. Expect less than the other.

— Anon.

~

Love gives and forgives. Self gets and forgets.

— Anon.

~

Do the things which people say you can't do.

— Napoleon Bonaparte

~

The best executive is the one who has sense enough to pick good men to do what he wants them to do, and self-restraint enough to keep from meddling with them while they do it.

— Theodore Roosevelt

~

A little difference between promises and memories.
Promises: We break them. Memories: They break us.

— Anon

~

If you pray, you will believe. If you believe, you will love. If
you love, you will help.

— Anon.

~

If you want to be great, you must work with great people.

— Jeyakrishnan

~

If you are a servant to your heart, then you will be the king of
the world.

— Anon.

~

There are two great days in a person's life: The day we were
born and the day when we prove why!

— William Barclay

~

If you desire to blossom like a rose in the garden, you have to
learn the art of adjusting with thorns.

— Anon.

~

Experience makes one modified. Training makes one
qualified. But involvement alone makes everyone satisfied.

— Anon.

~

'Delay' is the enemy of efficiency. 'Waiting' is the enemy of utilisation. So, don't delay anything and don't wait for anything.

— Anon.

~

In any moment of decision, the best thing you can do is the right thing, the next best thing is the wrong thing, and the worst thing you can do is nothing.

— Theodore Roosevelt

~

In a day, when you don't come across any problem — you can be sure that you are travelling in the wrong path.

— Swami Vivekananda

~

If you can solve your problem, then what is the need of worrying? If you can't solve it, then what is the use of worrying?

— Shantideva

~

Work out your own salvation. Do not depend on others.

— Gautama Buddha

~

The journey of a thousand miles starts with one step.

— Lao Tzu

~

One machine can do the work of fifty ordinary men. No machine can do the work of one extraordinary man.

— Elbert G Hubbard

~

Mental slums are more dangerous than material slums.

— Dr S Radhakrishnan

~

Good management is the art of making difficult things simple, not simple things difficult.

— Anon.

~

He who gains a victory over other men is strong, but he who gains a victory over himself is all powerful.

— Lao Tzu

~

The best day – today
The greatest sin – fear
The best gift – forgiveness
The meanest feeling – jealousy
The greatest need – common sense
The most expensive indulgence – hate
The greatest trouble maker – talking too much
The greatest teacher – one who makes you want to learn
The cleverest man – one who does what he thinks right
The worst bankrupt – the soul that has lost its enthusiasm

The cheapest, stupidest, easiest thing to do – finding fault
The best part of anyone's religion – gentleness and cheerfulness.

— Anon.

~

Do all the good you can,
By all the means you can,
In all the ways you can,
In all the places you can,
At all the times you can.
To all the people you can,
As long as ever you can.

— John Wesley

~

Only the actions of the just smell sweet and blossom in their dust.

— James Shirly

~

Judge not, that ye be not judged.

— The Bible

~

You must always be cheerful. You must cultivate this virtue again and again. Laughter and cheerfulness increase the circulation of the blood.

— Swami Sivananda

~

You have to go beyond your limitations and recognise yourself as the Absolute Being, through purity, devotion, aspiration and meditation.

— *Swami Sivananda*

~

Every breath that flows in the nose, every beat that throbs in the heart, every artery that pulsates in the body, every thought that arises in the mind, speaks to you that god is near.

— *Swami Sivananda*

~

A really sweet man is divine. He does not expect anything from others. He brings joy to others by his innate sweetness.

— *Anon.*

~

Youth are not useless; they are used less.

— *Swami Chinmayananda*

~

Extending one hand to help somebody has more value rather than joining two hands for prayer.

— *Anon.*

~

If an egg is broken by an outside force, a life ends. If an egg breaks from within, a life begins.

— *Anon.*

~

Talent should be like the spider's web. It may not be strong enough to hold this whole world but it should hold you to rule your kingdom.

— Jeyakrishnan

~

If you can't be a pencil to write anyone's happiness, then try at least to be a nice rubber to erase everyone's sorrows.

— Anon.

~

What is forgiveness? It is the sweet scent that a flower gives and the sweet juice an apple gives even when they are crushed. Be a forgiver always.

— Anon.

~

Real tears are not those that fall from the eyes and cover the face, but those that fall from the heart and cover the soul.

— Anon.

~

All beautiful things start from the heart. All bad things start from the mind. Never let the mind rule your heart. Let the heart rule your life.

— Anon.

~

The tongue is a dangerous animal kept inside the cage called the mouth. Don't open the cage unless it is absolutely necessary.

— A Chinese proverb

~

Satisfy the person who expects from you rather than surprising the person who never expected anything from you.

— Anon.

~

Don't lower your expectations to meet your performance. Raise your level of performance to meet your expectations. Expect the best of yourself and then do what is necessary to make it a reality.

— Ralph Marston

~

The most selfish one-letter word – I – Avoid it
The most satisfactory two-letter word – We – Use it
The most poisonous three-letter word – Ego – Kill it
The most used four-letter word – Love– Value it
The most pleasing five-letter word – Smile – Keep it
The most undesirable six-letter word – Rumour – Ignore it
The most hardworking seven-letter word – Success – Achieve it
The most enviable eight-letter word – Jealousy – Distance it
The most powerful nine-letter word – Knowledge – Acquire it
The most divine ten-letter word – Friendship – Maintain it.

— Anon.

~

Separation is a wound that no one can heal. But remembrance is a gift that no one can steal.

— Anon.

~

Love is the oil you put in the lamp of knowledge.

— Rig Veda

~

A secret is something which a person tells everybody not to tell anybody.

— Jeyakrishnan

~

Heartbeats are the biggest hypocrites in the world. They beat in our body but always dance to the tune of someone else.

— Anon.

~

Let your talk be such as is worthy of belief and your words be such as are commonly used.

— Ovid

~

Great spirits have always encountered violent opposition from mediocre minds.

— Albert Einstein

~

A diamond is merely a lump of coal that did well under pressure.

— Anon.

~

Good Relations

A star has five ends. A square has four ends. A triangle has three ends. A line has two ends. Life has one end. But good relations have no end.

— Anon.

~

The relations which require effort to be maintained are never strong and those that never require any effort to be maintained are indeed strong.

— Anon.

~

Please do not barge into my space. Stay close enough and enjoy the warmth. Too much of barging into my space will burn the relationship, sooner or later.

— Anon.

~

Death is not the greatest loss in life. The greatest loss is when a relationship dies inside us while we are alive.

— Anon.

~

Absence must be long enough so that somebody misses you. But it should not be so long that somebody learns to live without you!

— Anon.

~

To know when to go away and when to come closer is the key to any lasting relationship.

— Doménico Cieri Estrada

~

Love and respect will make any good relationship better.

— Stephen Ramjewan

~

Our greatest joy and our greatest pain comes in our relationships with others.

— Stephen R Covey

~

The fundamental glue that holds any relationship together is trust.

— Brian Tracy

~

Gratitude

Never look at what you have lost. Look at what you are left with. Gratitude gives you the power to survive.

— Prof Ranganathan

~

Feeling gratitude and not expressing it is like wrapping a present and not giving it.

— William Arthur Ward

~

Gratitude is not only the greatest of virtues, but also the parent of all the others.

— Marcus Tullius Cicero

~

Gratitude is the fairest blossom which springs from the soul.

— Henry Ward Beecher

~

Happiness

The only thing in the world which will increase in size after sharing it, is happiness.

— Anon.

~

The key to happiness is not that you never get angry, frustrated, or depressed. It's how quickly you decide to get out of it!

— Anon.

~

Worrying doesn't reduce yesterday's sorrows, but it empties today's strength. So don't worry. Stay happy and keep smiling.

— Anon.

~

If you wait for happiness, you will wait forever. But if you start being happy, you will be happy forever.

— Jeyakrishnan

~

The happiest people on this planet are not those who live for themselves but those who change themselves for the ones they love.

— Jeyakrishnan

~

Happiness is not something you plan for the future. It's something you design for the present. Make each moment a happy one.

— Anon.

~

Joy can be real only if people look upon their life as a service.

— Leo Nikalaevich Tolstoy

~

No one is born happy but everyone is born with the ability to create happiness.

— Anon.

~

The happiness of your life depends on the quality of your thoughts.

— Marcus Aurelius

~

Don't confuse comfort with happiness.

— Anon.

~

Peaceful surroundings cannot create happiness in you. But your happiness can create peaceful surroundings for those around you.

— *Jeyakrishnan*

~

When we are born, we cry and when we die, others cry. Make sure you have ample reasons to be cheerful between the two phases of crying.

— *Jeyakrishnan*

~

Accept what you cannot change. Change what you cannot accept. That is the key to being happy in life.

— *Jeyakrishnan*

~

Work is the key to happiness.

— *Anon.*

~

Call no man happy till he dies.

— *Aeschylus*

~

Hard Work

Hard work is like a cup of milk. Luck is just like a spoon of sugar. God always gives sugar to those who have a cup of milk!

— Anon.

~

Hard work is like the stairs. Luck is like a lift. A lift may fail but you always have the stairs to take you to the top.

— Anon.

~

Don't judge each day by the harvest you reap, but by the seeds you plant.

— Robert Louis Stevenson

~

Every day do something that will inch you closer to a better tomorrow.

— Doug Firebaugh

~

Every job is a self-portrait of the person who does it. Autograph your work with excellence.

— *Anon.*

~

Failure is not the worst thing in the world. The very worst is not to try.

— *Anon.*

~

Do every act of your life as if it were your last.

— *Marcus Aurelius*

~

People working hard are the assets of the nation and people working hardly are the liabilities of the nation.

— *SK Nazer*

~

There are no gains without pains.

— *Adlai Stevenson*

~

Hope

A human can live for forty days without food, three days without water, eight minutes without air. But he cannot live one second without hope. So never lose hope.

— Anon.

~

One can count the number of seeds in an apple, but one cannot count the number of apples in a seed. The future is unseen. Always hope for the best.

— Anon.

~

Where the willingness is great, the difficulties cannot be great.

— Niccolo Machiavelli

~

I am always doing things I can't do. That's how I get to do them.

— Pablo Picasso

~

Knowledge

Thinking is progress. Non-thinking is stagnation of the individual, organisation and the country. Thinking leads to action. Knowledge without action is useless and irrelevant. Knowledge with action converts adversity into prosperity.

— *Dr APJ Abdul Kalam*

~

If you learn only methods, you'll be tied to your methods. But if you learn principles, you can devise your own methods and do something greater.

— *Dr Sivaraman*

~

The doorstep to the temple of wisdom is a knowledge of our own ignorance.

— *Benjamin Franklin*

~

Ignorance is the curse of god; knowledge is the wing wherewith we fly to heaven.

— *William Shakespeare*

~

To know is to know that you know nothing. That is the meaning of true knowledge.

— *Confucius*

~

Knowledge becomes evil if the aim be not virtuous.

— *Plato*

~

If money is your hope for independence you will never have it. The real security that a man will have in this world is a reserve of knowledge, experience and ability.

— *Henry Ford*

~

Knowledge is borrowed from god.
Repayment is service to humanity.

— *SK Nazer*

~

Leadership

A leaf which falls from the tree is at the mercy of the wind. It goes wherever the wind takes it. Be the wind to drive others and not the leaf to be driven by others.

— *Anon.*

~

Leadership has a harder job to do than just to choose sides. It must bring sides together.

— *Jesse Jackson*

~

I suppose leadership at one time meant muscles; but today it means getting along with people.

— *MK Gandhi*

~

It is better to lead from behind and to put others in front, especially when you celebrate victory when nice things occur. You take the front line when there is danger. Then people will appreciate your leadership.

— *Nelson Mandela*

~

Management is doing things right; leadership is doing the right things.

— Peter Drucker

~

A good objective of leadership is to help those who are doing poorly to do well and to help those who are doing well to do even better.

— Jim Rohn

~

Leadership is solving problems. The day soldiers stop bringing you their problems is the day you have stopped leading them. They have either lost confidence that you can help or concluded you do not care. Either case is a failure of leadership.

— Colin Powell

~

Leadership is the art of getting someone else to do something you want done because he wants to do it.

— Dwight D Eisenhower

~

The supreme quality for leadership is unquestionably integrity. Without it, no real success is possible, no matter whether it is on a section gang, a football field, in an army, or in an office.

— Dwight D Eisenhower

~

You don't lead by hitting people over the head — that's assault, not leadership.

— *Dwight D Eisenhower*

~

No institution can possibly survive if it needs geniuses or supermen to manage it. It must be organised in such a way as to be able to get along under a leadership composed of average human beings.

— *Peter Drucker*

~

I have a different vision of leadership. A leadership is someone who brings people together.

— *George W Bush*

~

Leadership to me means duty, honour, country. It means character, and it means listening from time to time.

— *George W Bush*

~

Effective leadership is putting first things first. Effective management is discipline, carrying it out.

— *Stephen R Covey*

~

Management is efficiency in climbing the ladder of success; leadership determines whether the ladder is leaning against the right wall.

— *Stephen R Covey*

~

Good leadership consists of showing average people how to do the work of superior people.

— *John D Rockefeller*

~

I forgot to shake hands and be friendly. It was an important lesson about leadership.

— *Lee Iacocca*

~

Character matters; leadership descends from character.

— *Rush Limbaugh*

~

Don't necessarily avoid sharp edges. Occasionally they are necessary to leadership.

— *Donald Rumsfeld*

~

Leadership is getting someone to do what they don't want to do, to achieve what they want to achieve.

— *Tom Landry*

~

Leadership is a matter of having people look at you and gain confidence, seeing how you react. If you're in control, they're in control.

— *Tom Landry*

~

Learning

The joy of a book is in the pages you haven't read.
The glory of your life is in the days yet to be lived.

— Dr APJ Adbul Kalam

~

Sometimes, failure is needed to know; loss is needed to gain;
because some lessons are best when learnt through pain.

— Anon.

~

If a child lives with criticism, he learns to condemn.
If a child lives with hostility, he learns to fight.
If a child lives with shame, he learns to feel guilty.
If a child lives with tolerance, he learns to be patient.
If a child lives with praise, he learns to appreciate.
If a child lives with fairness, he learns to be just.
If a child lives with security, he learns to have faith.
If a child lives with approval, he learns to like himself.
If a child lives with acceptance, he learns to find love.

— Dorothy L Law

~

Life

Anyone who keeps learning stays young. The greatest thing in life is to keep your mind young.

— Henry Ford

~

One of the greatest illusions of life is that we always believe there is more time tomorrow than today.

— Anon.

~

Life is at its weakest, when there are more doubts than trust. But life is at its strongest, when you learn how to trust in spite of the doubts.

— Anon.

~

Life is a book of mystery. You never know which chapter will bring a good twist. Continue reading because happiness comes when it is most unexpected.

— Swaran Singh

~

Keep in the heart things which hurt others. But never try to hurt others by keeping something in your heart.

— *Anon.*

~

Life should be like running water. When one side of its flow is blocked, it continues its journey by flowing down the other side. Don't stop your journey with one failure.

— *Anon.*

~

Birth was not our choice. Death will not be our choice but the way we live our life is our choice. Make the best of this choice.

— *Anon.*

~

Life is a ticket to the greatest show on the earth.

— *Anon.*

~

Life is an echo; everything comes back – the good, the bad, the false, the true. So give the best you have and the best will come back to you!

— *Anon.*

~

Communication will win you the outer world. Silence will win you the inner world. Holistic living lies in winning both the worlds.

— *Anon.*

~

Life is all about three things. Winning, losing and sharing. Winning others' hearts, losing bad habits and sharing happy moments.

— Anon.

~

A beautiful life does not just happen. It is cultivated every day in prayer, humility, sacrifice, love, affection and good deeds.

— Jeyakrishnan

~

Every day is a renewal, every morning is a miracle. The joy you feel is life.

— Anon.

~

A life spent in making mistakes is not only more honourable, but more useful than a life spent doing nothing.

— GB Shaw

~

Life will be pleasant, if we are satisfied with what we have. But it will be more thrilling if we make efforts to achieve what we desire!

— Jeyakrishnan

~

Two things in life should always be remembered.
1. Don't take any decision when you are angry.
2. Don't make any promises when you are happy!

— Anon.

~

Life is like a novel. It is filled with suspense. You have no idea what is going to happen next until you turn the page.

— *Sidney Sheldon*

~

Life never turns the way we want. But we live it the best way we can. There's no perfect life, but we can fill it with perfect moments.

— *Anon.*

~

Life is like a flowing river of opportunities. It's upto you to stand up with a bucket or with a spoon!

— *Anon.*

~

Life comes only once. Enjoy it to the fullest. Never be angry or sad because for every second of anger or sadness, you lose sixty micro-seconds of happiness.

— *Jeyakrishnan*

~

Change is the nature of life! But challenge is an aim of life! So always challenge the changes, do not change the challenges.

— *Anon.*

~

Every king was once a crying baby and every great building was once a blueprint. It's not where you are today, but where you will reach tomorrow. That's life.

— Anon.

~

The earth weighs 6.6 septillion tonnes. Don't make it heavier by carrying a heavier heart! Stay light. Laugh often. Love your life.

— Anon.

~

A butterfly lives only for a few days, still it flies joyfully capturing many hearts. Each moment in life is precious, live every moment to the fullest.

— Anon.

~

Like water, be peaceful. Like the earth, be balanced. Like fire, be bright. Like the wind, fly free of problems. Life is beautiful. Live and enjoy it.

— Anon.

~

The best moments in life: Lying in bed and listening to the rain outside. Thinking about the person you love. Taking a long drive on a calm road. Finding money in your old jeans when you need it. Holding hands with someone you love.

— Anon.

~

Accepting every victory with a humble heart and every defeat with a gracious mind is the best way to live in this world.

— Jeyakrishnan

~

Life is travelled only once. Today's moments become tomorrow's memories. Enjoy every moment, good or bad, because the gift of life is life itself.

— Anon.

~

An arrow can be shot only by dragging it backwards. So whenever life pulls us back, let us not worry. It's going to lead us ahead with immense force.

— DJ Bethelraj

~

Life is like glass; handle it with care.

— Anon.

~

Beautiful life is just an imagination. But life is more beautiful than imagination.

— Anon.

~

The biggest suspense of life is we know for whom we are living but we never know the person who is living for us.

— Anon.

~

Every painful moment is a gift of god to make you unique. So face the pains to become the best in your life in front of others.

— *Osho*

~

Life is like a chess game. There should not be any move without valid reason. Once you make a wrong move, it's very difficult to get back.

— *Anon.*

~

Life is no 'brief candle' for me. It is a sort of splendid torch which I have got hold of for a moment; and I want to make it burn as brightly as possible before handing it on to future generations.

— *GB Shaw*

~

Everyone is trying to accomplish something big, not realising that life is made up of little things.

— *Frank Howard Clark*

~

Life is what happens to you while you're busy making other plans.

— *John Lennon*

~

The most important thing in the Olympics is not winning but taking part. The essential thing in life is not conquering but fighting well.

— *Pierre de Coubertin*

~

A person tired of his life's trials and hardships, asked god, 'Why are there so many mountains to climb in life?' God replied, 'For you to have a better view! Live and love life.'

— *Anon.*

~

They say it takes a minute to find a special person, an hour to appreciate him, a day to love him but then an entire life to forget him.

— *Anon.*

~

We work for making a better tomorrow but when tomorrow comes, instead of enjoying again we start thinking of a better tomorrow.

— *Anon.*

~

Mistakes are a part of life. The only person who never makes mistakes is the one who does nothing. Learn from your mistakes.

— *Adam Smith*

~

Life is a flower of which love is the nectar.

— *Anon.*

~

Light

Love dispels hatred. Light dispels darkness. Service dispels selfishness. Knowledge dispels ignorance. Let your light shine to dispel hatred, darkness, selfishness and ignorance.

— Jeyakrishnan

~

Darkness cannot drive out darkness; only light can do that. Hate cannot drive out hate; only love can do that.

— Martin Luther King, Jr

~

Walking with a friend in the dark is better than walking alone in the light.

— Helen Keller

~

It is better to light a candle than curse the darkness.

— A Chinese proverb

~

Living

Man can fly like a bird, sing like a cuckoo, dance like a peacock, swim like a fish. But always, man cannot live like a man.

— *Swami Vivekananda*

~

Art is not living. It is the use of living.

— *Audre Lorde*

~

Real living is living for others.

— *Bruce Lee*

~

This life is worth living, we can say, since it is what we make it.

— *William James*

~

Live life in the most beautiful way, with the person who loves you the most. Because if that person has 100 reasons to smile, 99 are because of you.

— *Jeyakrishnan*

~

Love

Hate but love more. Argue but agree more. Talk but listen more. Punish but forgive more. Then people will love you more than you love them.

— Jeyakrishnan

~

I have two eyes but can't see you every day. I have two ears but can't hear your voice every day. But I have one little heart that remembers you every day.

— Anon.

~

Life teaches you to love and also teaches you to cry. It may be ironic but it's true that you can't know the value of love until you cry for it.

— Anon.

~

Love is the whole history of a woman's life, it is but an episode in a man's.

— Madame de Stael

~

Those we love never go away, they walk beside us every day: unseen and unheard, still near, still loved, still missed and still very dear.

— Anon.

~

Love isn't finding someone you can live with. It's finding someone you can't live without.

— Anon.

~

Love is an endless mystery, for it has nothing else to explain it.

— Rabindranath Tagore

~

Love is the immortal flow of energy that nourishes, extends and preserves. Its eternal goal is life.

— Smiley Blanton

~

True love thinks of no evil and asks nothing in return for itself, it imputes no motive and sees only the bright side of things.

— Swami Sivananda

~

It is love that really sustains life.

— Swami Sivananda

~

Love in action is what gives us grace.

— Mother Teresa

~

Mind

Mind is like a parachute. It works only when it is open.

— *Anthony J D'Angelo*

~

Do not dwell in the past, do not dream of the future, concentrate the mind on the present moment.

— *Gautama Buddha*

~

The mind is everything. What you think, you become.

— *Gautama Buddha*

~

We are shaped by our thoughts; we become what we think. When the mind is pure, joy follows like a shadow that never leaves.

— *Gautama Buddha*

~

Age is an issue of mind over matter. If you don't mind, it doesn't matter.

— *Mark Twain*

~

Patience

The mind is the most powerful thing in the world. One who has controlled his mind can control anything in this world.

— *Anon.*

~

Even a big pot full of water will be emptied by a small hole; just a little anger or ego will burn the nobility of a good heart. Be cool always.

— *Anon.*

~

Be patient and understanding. Life is too short to be vengeful or malicious.

— *Phillips Brooks*

~

Good character is not formed in a week or a month. It is created little by little, day by day. Protracted and patient effort is needed to develop good character.

— *Heraclitus*

~

Peace

A man asked God, 'I want peace.' God replied, 'Remove the 'I' that is ego; remove the 'want' that is desire and 'peace' will be automatically yours.'

— Anon.

~

Since wars begin in the minds of men, it is in the minds of men that the defences of peace must be constructed.

— UNESCO Constitution

~

Peace cannot be kept by force; it can only be achieved by understanding.

— Albert Einstein

~

When the power of love overcomes the love of power, the world will know peace.

— Jimi Hendrix

~

It is an unfortunate fact that we can secure peace only by preparing for war.

— John F Kennedy

~

Peace begins with a smile.

— Mother Teresa

~

Be at war with your vices, at peace with your neighbours.

— Benjamin Franklin

~

Peace begins where ambition ends.
Peace brings joy; money brings war.
If you want peace, prepare for war.

— Anon.

~

The result of war is peace.

— St Augustine

~

People

Cheerful people are like sunlight. They shine into the corners of the heart and offer bright mornings and fresh hopes.

— Anon.

~

There are two types of people in the world — those who leave a mark and those who leave a stain.

— Anon.

~

People are made to be loved and things are made to be used. The problem is: people are being used and things are being loved.

— Anon.

~

He who has a thousand friends has not a friend to spare and he who has one enemy shall meet him everywhere.

— Anon.

~

He who would be great must be fervent in his prayers, fearless in his principles, firm in his purposes and faithful in his promises.

— *Jeyakrishnan*

~

People are hated for a single mistake, even though there are a thousand reasons to love them.

— *Anon.*

~

Love both your friend and your enemy. The friend will be the support for success. The enemy will be the reason for success.

— *Anon.*

~

Wonderful people are carefully created by god, wonderful moments are carefully planned by god and wonderful persons are carefully gifted by god.

— *Jeyakrishnan*

~

What happens to good people when bad things happen to them? They become better people.

— *Anon.*

~

An opportunist is one who starts taking a bath when he accidentally falls into a river.

— *Anon.*

~

If people talk behind your back, what does that mean? Simple. It means you are two steps ahead of them. So don't worry. Enjoy life.

— Jeyakrishnan

~

To make a man happy, understand him a lot and love him a little. To make a woman happy, understand her a little and love her a lot.

— Anon.

~

Losers visualise the penalties of failure. Winners visualise the rewards of success.

— Anon.

~

Good people do not need laws to tell them to act responsibly, while bad people will find a way around the laws.

— Plato

~

To speak and to offend some people, are but one and the same thing.

— La Bruyere

~

Listen to those who themselves are good listeners.

— Anon.

~

Be not afraid of greatness: some are born great, some achieve greatness and some have greatness thrust upon them.

— William Shakespeare

~

For some, there is never a solution moment. For some others, there is never a problem moment.

— Jeyakrishnan

~

Those who would give up Essential Liberty to purchase a little Temporary Safety, deserve neither Liberty nor Safety.

— Benjamin Franklin

~

Being a good person is like being a goalkeeper — no matter how many goals we saved, people will remember only the ones we missed!

— Anon.

~

Healthy people are nation's assets.

— Jawaharlal Nehru

~

The wrong kind of people dislike you for the good in you and the right kind of people love you knowing even the bad in you.

— Anon.

~

Perseverance

Many fail because they do not realise how close they were to success when they gave up. Never give up until you reach your goal.

— Thomas Alva Edison

~

If you can't fly, run. If you can't run, walk. If you can't walk, crawl. But whatever you do, you have to keep moving forward.

— Martin Luther King, Jr

~

A sunset here is a sunrise on the other end of the world. We should never give up because what appears to be the end may actually be a new beginning.

— Anon.

~

Perseverance is failing nineteen times and succeeding on the twentieth.

— Julie Andrews

~

If your plans have failed, ask yourself if there is a better plan waiting to be discovered.

— *Anon.*

~

The duck looks smooth and calm on top, but underneath there is restless paddling. Similarly in life, nothing worthwhile comes without a struggle.

— *Anon.*

~

Perseverance is not a long race; it is many short races one after another.

— *Walter Elliott*

~

Success is not final, failure is not fatal: it is the courage to continue that counts.

— *Winston Churchill*

~

A righteous man falls seven times, and rises again.

— *The Bible*

~

Philanthropy

We make a living by what we get, but we make a life by what we give. Develop the habit of giving unconditionally. God will give you back in abundance.

— Dr Agnes

~

Let us work like a well-oiled machine to serve the poor from their lot by delivering them from the curse of illiteracy and poverty.

— Indira Gandhi

~

Human enterprise can achieve meaningful progress only when it gives honest expression to its innate sense of social care and commitment.

— Jeyakrishnan

~

Recall the face of the poorest and weakest man you have seen and ask yourself if the step you contemplate is going to be of any use to him.

— MK Gandhi

~

Pleasure

The great pleasure in life is doing what people say you cannot do.

— Walter Bagehot

~

The noblest pleasure is the joy of understanding.

— Leonardo da Vinci

~

Most men pursue pleasure with such breathless haste that they hurry past it.

— Soren Kierkegaard

~

There is no pleasure in having nothing to do; the fun is having lots to do and not doing it.

— Mary Wilson Little

~

Men of leisure are men of pleasure.

— Anon.

~

Prayers

It's wonderful to get answers to prayer but it's even more wonderful to mould yourself and become an answer to somebody's prayer!

— Anon.

~

The saline water of the ocean evaporates and falls from above as pure drinking water in the form of rain. Likewise, when prayers go up, they pour down in their purest form as blessings.

— Anon.

~

God is not a cosmic bellboy for whom we can press a button to get things.

— Harry Emerson Fosdick

~

More things are wrought by prayer than this world dreams of.

— Alfred Tennyson

~

The shortest solution to every problem is to minimise the distance between your knees and the floor. Those who kneel down to god can stand up to anything.

— Anon.

~

God sometimes delays His help to test our faith and energise our prayers. Our boat may be tossed while He sleeps but He wakes up before it sinks.

— Anon.

~

Courage is fear that has said its prayers.

— Dorothy Bernard

~

Prayer is the voice of faith.

— William Van Horne

~

Present

Never think more about the past; it brings tears.
Don't think more about the future; it brings fears.
Live this second; it brings cheers.

— Anon.

~

Losers live in the past. Winners learn from the past and enjoy working in the present towards a happy future.

— Denis Waitley

~

If we open a quarrel between the past and the present, we shall find that we have lost the future.

— Winston Churchill

~

Change is the law of life. And those who look only to the past or present are certain to miss the future.

— John F Kennedy

~

There's no present. There's only the immediate future and the recent past.

~

Who controls the past controls the future. Who controls the present controls the past.

— George Orwell

~

It takes a long time to bring the past up to the present.

— Franklin D Roosevelt

~

Happiness is not something you postpone for the future; it is something you design for the present.

— Jim Rohn

~

Sometimes the past seems too big for the present to hold.

— Chuck Palahniuk

~

Yesterday is history, tomorrow is a mystery, today is god's gift, that's why we call it the present.

— Joan Rivers

~

Prudence

No need to complain about others; just change yourself. It is easier to protect our feet with shoes than to carpet the whole world.

— Anon.

~

One should keep one's eyes wide open before marriage and half-shut afterwards.

— Benjamin Franklin

~

No one ever won a game of chess by betting only on each forward move. Sometimes you have to move backward to get a better step forward.

— Amar Gopal Bose

~

The shortest way to do many things is to do one thing at a time.

— Anon.

~

Punctuality

Punctuality is not about valuing time but about valuing commitment.

— Jeyakrishnan

~

I never could have done what I have done without the habits of punctuality, order, and diligence, without the determination to concentrate myself on one subject at a time.

— Charles Dickens

~

Punctuality is one of the cardinal business virtues: always insist on it in your subordinates.

— Don Marquis

~

Punctuality is the politeness of kings.

— Louis XVIII

~

Purpose

In the race between a cat and a mouse, the mouse mostly wins because the cat is running for its food and the mouse for its life. Remember, purpose is more important than need.

— *Anon.*

~

Understand how beautifully god has added one more day in your life, not because you need it but because someone else needs you!

— *Anon.*

~

Success demands singleness of purpose.

— *Vince Lombardi*

~

Efforts and courage are not enough without purpose and direction.

— *John F Kennedy*

~

Reality

Healthy children are a nation's assets.

— Dr APJ Abdul Kalam

~

Do not act without thinking and do not keep thinking without acting.

— Jeyakrishnan

~

Stop dreaming and face reality. Keep dreaming and make it a reality.

— Kristian Kan

~

Be realistic about your dreams and try to transform them into reality if they are good. Realistic goals are encouraging and build high self-esteem.

— Anon.

~

When a man and a woman are married, their romance ceases and their history commences.

— Anon.

~

The biggest lie on the planet: When I get what I want, I will be happy.

— Anon.

~

Failure means delay, not defeat.

— Anon.

~

Wealth can't buy health but health can buy wealth.

— Anon.

~

The best investment on the earth is the earth.

— Louis J Glickman

~

A dream you dream alone is only a dream. A dream you dream together is reality.

— John Lennon

~

Man, alone, has the power to transform his thoughts into physical reality; man, alone, can dream and make his dreams come true.

— Napoleon Hill

~

Reason

Nothing happens without a reason. A person who has come into your life has come either to teach you something or to learn something from you.

— Anon.

~

The only reason for time is so that everything doesn't happen at once.

— Albert Einstein

~

One should always be in love. That is the reason one should never marry.

— Oscar Wilde

~

Anger is never without a reason, but seldom with a good one.

— Benjamin Franklin

~

If passion drives you, let reason hold the reins.

— Benjamin Franklin

~

Religion

We have enough religion to make us hate, but not enough to make us love one another.

— Jonathan Swift

~

Religion is the idol of the mob; it adores everything it does not understand.

— Frederick the Great

~

Science without religion is lame, religion without science is blind.

— Albert Einstein

~

I love you when you bow in your mosque, kneel in your temple, pray in your church.
For you and I are sons of one religion, and it is the spirit.

— Khalil Gibran

~

Just as a candle cannot burn without fire, men cannot live without a spiritual life.

— Gautama Buddha

~

Respect

Respect your child's emotions. Never trespass on his or her solitude.

— Anon.

~

Success can be achieved. Fame can be attracted. Glory can be won. Respect can only be earned.

— Anon.

~

We do not covet anything from any nation except their respect.

— Winston Churchill

~

Knowledge will give you power, but character respect.

— Bruce Lee

~

Nothing is more despicable than respect based on fear.

— Albert Camus

~

Reverence

We are not only grateful to our teachers who taught us at school but also grateful to all other people from whom we learn something every day.

— Jeyakrishnan

~

Ethics is nothing else than reverence for life.

— Albert Schweitzer

~

If a man loses his reverence for any part of life, he will lose his reverence for all of life.

— Albert Schweitzer

~

Spend enough time around success and failure, and you learn a reverence for possibility.

— Dale Dauten

~

Sacrifice

Great things can be done by great sacrifices only.

— Jaggi Vasudev

~

He profits most who sacrifices best.

— Jeyakrishnan

~

Compromise is but the sacrifice of one right or good in the hope of retaining another — too often ending in the loss of both.

— Tryon Edwards

~

Great achievement is usually born of great sacrifice, and is never the result of selfishness.

— Napoleon Hill

~

Silence

Hundred hard words do not give pain but a true friend's silence brings more tears.

— Jeyakrishnan

~

Our lives begin to end the day we become silent about the things that matter.

— Martin Luther King, Jr

~

A seed, while growing, makes no noise. A tree, while falling makes noise. Destruction is noisy. Creation is always quiet.

— Anon.

~

A man who lives right, and is right, has more power in his silence than another has by his words.

— Phillips Brooks

~

Smile

Love is the language even the deaf can hear.
Smile is the language even the dumb can speak.

— Mother Teresa

~

It does not mean that a man who is always smiling has no problems. But he has the ability to overcome all problems.

— Anon.

~

Life can give us a hundred reasons to cry. But god gives us a thousand reasons to smile. So, smile forever!

— Anon.

~

Living in favourable and unfavourable situations is part of living. But smiling in all those situations is called the art of living.

— Anon.

~

Smile is a source to win a heart.

— Anon.

~

Smile to end the day.
Pray to bless your sleep.
Sing to lighten your dreams.

— Anon.

~

Smile will be complete when it begins with your heart, reflects in your eyes and ends with a glow on your face.

— Anon.

~

Anger is a condition in which the tongue works faster than the mind. Smile is an action which makes everything work faster except the tongue. So keep smiling.

— Jeyakrishnan

~

A smiling face is good recommendation.

— Anon.

~

What is the difference between your smile and my smile? You smile when you feel happy and I smile when I see you happy.

— Anon.

~

Smile takes you a mile closer to god.

— Jeyakrishnan

~

Sometimes your joy is the source of your smile but sometimes your smile can be the source of your joy.

— *Thich Naht Hanh*

~

We smile at whom we like; we cry for whom we care; we laugh with whom we enjoy.

— *Anon.*

~

A pure-hearted person can have a wonderful smile that makes even his enemy feel guilty for being his enemy. So win the world with your smile.

— *Anon.*

~

Always be happy, always wear a smile, not because life is full of reasons to smile but your smile itself is a reason for others to smile.

— *Jeyakrishnan*

~

A smile is a curve which can set a lot of things straight.

— *Anon.*

~

You will smile when you think of the moments when you cried. You will cry when you think of the moments when you smiled.

— *Anon.*

~

Speech

The manner of your speaking is full as important as the matter, as more people have ears to be tickled, than understandings to judge.

— Lord Chesterfield

~

Let your speech be always with grace, seasoned with salt, that you may know how you ought to answer every man.

— The Bible

~

Speak clearly, if you speak at all.
Carve every word before you let it fall.

— Oliver Wendell Holmes

~

The wise man, before he speaks, will consider well what he speaks, to whom he speaks and where and when.

— St Ambrose

~

A great thing is a great book, but greater than all is the talk of a great man.

— Benjamin Disraeli

~

Strength

Strength does not come from physical capacity. It comes from an indomitable will.

— MK Gandhi

~

The difference between a successful person and others is not a lack of strength, not a lack of knowledge, but rather a lack of will.

— Vince Lombardi

~

Faith is the strength by which a shattered world shall emerge into the light.

— Helen Keller

~

Good actions give strength to ourselves and inspire good actions in others.

— Plato

~

Strength and growth come only through continuous effort and struggle.

— Napoleon Hill

~

Unity is strength: when there is teamwork and collaboration, wonderful things can be achieved.

— *Mattie Stepanek*

~

The real man smiles in trouble, gathers strength from distress, and grows brave by reflection.

— *Thomas Paine*

~

Strength does not come from winning. Your struggles develop your strength. When you go through hardships and decide not to surrender, that is strength.

— *Arnold Schwarzenegger*

~

The spirit of man is more important than mere physical strength, and the spiritual fibre of a nation than its wealth.

— *Dwight D Eisenhower*

~

Every great dream begins with a dreamer. Always remember, you have within you the strength, the patience, and the passion to reach for the stars to change the world.

— *Harriet Tubman*

~

Success

Read about success, speak about success, dream about success, think about success. That is the way to get success.

— *Dr APJ Abdul Kalam*

~

He who has truth and courage in his heart is the one who wins at the end.

— *Anon.*

~

The key to success is to set your own goals and determine your motivations. Life belongs to those who dare.

— *Shiv Khera*

~

What is success? Success is when your signature becomes an autograph.

— *Anon.*

~

Victory is not the property of the brilliant. It's the crown for those who bow themselves in front of hard work and confidence.

— *Anon.*

~

The world is waiting for you. Walk with your aims, run with confidence and fly with achievements. Reach the peak of success.

— Anon.

~

Fear is the main reason for every failure and confidence is the main reason for all successes. So, be confident. Success will come to you.

— Anon.

~

Success seems to be connected with action. Successful people keep moving. They make mistakes but they don't quit.

— Conrad Hilton

~

Success is to be measured not so much by the position that one has reached in life as by the obstacles which he has overcome while trying to succeed.

— Booker T Washington

~

Don't look back when you are moving towards success. But, don't forget to look back after reaching success.

— Jeyakrishnan

~

Self-trust is the first secret of success.

— Ralph Waldo Emerson

~

If you want to be successful, it's just simple: Know what you're doing, love what you're doing and believe in what you're doing.

— William Rogers

~

For a man of confidence, all roads lead to success. For a man of hard work, all success follows him on his road.

— Anon.

~

One cannot achieve success every time. It's all a part of the learning process.

— Amitabh Bachchan

~

All you need in this life is ignorance and confidence and then success is sure.

— Mark Twain

~

Success has a simple formula: do your best and people may like it.

— Anon.

~

If you fall, don't see the place where you fell but see the place where you slipped. Success is all about correcting your mistakes.

— Anon.

~

Successful people don't do great things. They do small things in a great way. They overcome obstacles to achieve their objectives.

— Anon.

~

Our greatest glory is not in never falling, but in rising every time we fall.

— Confucius

~

A successful man is one who can lay a firm foundation with the bricks others have thrown at him.

— David Brinkley

~

Failure is success if we learn from it.

— Malcolm Forbes

~

Don't aim for success if you want it; just do what you love and believe in, and it will come naturally.

— David Frost

~

Sympathy

The single finger which wipes tears during our failure is much better than the ten fingers which come together to clap for our victory.

— Anon.

~

Sympathy is the essence of love.

— SK Nazer

~

If there was less sympathy in the world, there would be less trouble in the world.

— Oscar Wilde

~

No one has yet realised the wealth of sympathy, the kindness and generosity hidden in the soul of a child. The effort of every true education should be to unlock that treasure.

— Emma Goldman

~

Teachers

The true teacher is he who can immediately come down to the level of the student and transfer his soul to the student.

— Swami Vivekananda

~

A beautiful picture is a silent teacher.

— The Author

~

One good schoolmaster is worth a thousand priests.

— Robert Green Ingersoll

~

The mediocre teacher tells. The good teacher explains. The great teacher inspires.

— William Arthur Ward

~

A good teacher must himself be a fellow traveller in the exciting pursuit of knowledge.

— Dr S Radhakrishnan

~

I seek a method by which teachers teach less and the learners learn more.

— Johann Comenius

~

Without mistakes we don't grow. Mistakes are our best teachers.

— Swami Vishnudevananda

~

Love is a better teacher than duty.

— Albert Einstein

~

It is the supreme art of the teacher to awaken joy in creative expression and knowledge.

— Albert Einstein

~

Experience is a dear teacher, but fools will learn at no other.

— Benjamin Franklin

~

In the practice of tolerance, one's enemy is the best teacher.

— Dalai Lama

~

Experience is the teacher of all things.

— Julius Caesar

~

Success is a lousy teacher. It seduces smart people into thinking they can't lose.

— *Bill Gates*

~

I like a teacher who gives you something to take home to think about besides homework.

— *Lily Tomlin*

~

If a country is to be corruption free and become a nation of beautiful minds, I strongly feel there are three key societal members who can make a difference. They are the father, the mother and the teacher.

— *Dr APJ Abdul Kalam*

~

I am indebted to my father for living, but to my teacher for living well.

— *Alexander the Great*

~

A teacher who is attempting to teach without inspiring the pupil with a desire to learn is hammering on cold iron.

— *Horace Mann*

~

Team

Team work is the fuel that allows common people to attain uncommon results.

— Anon.

~

Teams with different personalities are more productive than teams composed of compatible individuals.

— Robin Sharma

~

The speed of the boss is the speed of the team.

— Lee Iacocca

~

Finding good players is easy. Getting them to play as a team is another story.

— Casey Stengel

~

Tears

A tear coming out of the eyes is never a sign of weakness but a sign of care and love. We cry only for whom we love. Express yourself because tears are unspoken words.

— *Anon.*

~

Both tears and sweat are salty, but they render a different result. Tears will get you sympathy; sweat will get you change.

— *Jesse Jackson*

~

Certainly tears are given to us to use. Like all good gifts, they should be used properly.

— *Loretta Young*

~

Joy's smile is much closer to tears than laughter.

— *Victor Hugo*

~

Time

Time is like a river. You can't touch the same water twice because the flow that has passed will never pass again. Enjoy every moment of your life.

— *Anon.*

~

'Time' is a rare luxury which can never be purchased at any cost. So when someone spends it for you, it defines the depth of care he or she has for you.

— *Anon.*

~

The most wasted of all days is that in which we have not laughed.

— *Nicolas Chamfort*

~

The time to repair the roof is when the sun is shining.

— *John F Kennedy*

~

Time spent laughing is time spent with the gods.

— *A Japanese proverb*

~

In the primitive societies, nobody had a watch and everyone had time. But in the present societies, everyone has a watch but nobody has time.

— Sivakumar

~

If you can't be on time, be early.

— Anon.

~

Everything happens to everybody sooner or later if there is time enough.

— GB Shaw

~

Lose not yourself in a far off time, seize the moment that is thine.

— Friedrich Schiller

~

The future is something which everyone reaches at the rate of sixty minutes an hour, whatever he does, whoever he is.

— CS Lewis

~

Time = Life. Therefore, waste your time and waste your life, or master your time and master your life.

— Alan Lakein

~

Time does not change us. It just unfolds us.

— *Max Frisch*

~

Time is the coin of your life. It is the only coin you have, and only you can determine how it will be spent. Be careful lest you let other people spend it for you.

— *Carl Sandburg*

~

Time is the school in which we learn, time is the fire in which we burn.

— *Delmore Schwartz*

~

Time is the wisest counsellor of all.

— *Pericles*

~

Time is what we want most, but what we use worst.

— *William Penn*

~

Time makes heroes but dissolves celebrities.

— *Daniel J Boorstin*

~

Waste your money and you're only out of money, but waste your time and you've lost a part of your life.

— *Michael LeBoeuf*

~

Trust

Trusting a person is giving someone the ability to destroy you completely. But you still believe they won't.

— Anon.

~

Trusting in god won't make the mountain smaller but will make climbing easier. Don't ask him for a lighter load but ask him for a stronger shoulder.

— Anon.

~

When god solves your problems, you trust in His ability. If god doesn't solve your problems, He trusts in your ability!

— Anon.

~

Trust is like elastic stretched by two people. As long as both hold it, both will be happy. The moment one leaves it, the other feels terrible pain.

— Jeyakrishnan

~

Virtues

A clay pot having milk will be ranked higher than a golden pot having poison. Not our outer glamour but our inner virtues make us valuable.

— Anon.

~

One must say little things nobly because they are propped up by expression, tone and manner.

— La Bruyere

~

The superior man thinks always of virtue; the common man thinks of comfort.

— Confucius

~

Some rise by sin, and some by virtue fall.

— William Shakespeare

~

All the gold which is under or upon the earth is not enough to give in exchange for virtue.

— Plato

~

Vision

A blind person asked Mother Teresa: 'Can there be anything worse than losing your sight?'
She replied: 'Yes, losing your vision.'

— *Mother Teresa*

~

The only thing worse than being blind is having sight but no vision.

— *Helen Keller*

~

Vision is the art of seeing what is invisible to others.

— *Jonathan Swift*

~

Where there is no vision, there is no hope.

— *George Washington Carver*

~

Winning

Soft speech, clean heart, peaceful eyes, strong hands, focussed mind and determined decision with god's love always make you a winner.

— Anon.

~

I've missed more than 9000 shots in my career. I've lost almost 300 games. Twenty-six times, I've been trusted to take the game winning shot and missed. I've failed over and over and over again in my life. And that is why I succeed.

— Michael Jordan

~

Winning isn't everything, but the will to win is everything.

— Vince Lombardi

~

The momentous thing in human life is the art of winning the soul to good or evil.

— Pythagoras

~

Words

Kind words can be short and easy to speak but their echoes are truly endless.

— Mother Teresa

~

Words are the soul's ambassadors.

— James Howell

~

Words are, of course, the most powerful drug used by mankind.

— Rudyard Kipling

~

Heaven and earth shall pass away, but my words shall not pass away.

— The Bible

~

Words are the only things that last forever, they are more durable than the eternal hills.

— William Hazlitt

~

Every word man's lips have uttered echoes in god's skies.

— *Adelaide Anne Procter*

~

Loyal words have the secret of healing grief.

— *Menander*

~

A word in season spoken may calm the troubled breast.

— *Charles Jeffreys*

~

Apt words have power to assuage the tumours of a troubled mind.

— *John Milton*

~

Good words cool more than cold water.

— *John Ray*

~

Fair words never hurt the tongue.

— *George Chapman*

~

Soft words win hard hearts.

— *Anon.*

~

A blow with a word strikes deeper than a blow with a sword.

— *Robert Burton*

~

Sharp words make more wounds than surgeons can heal.

— Thomas Churchyard

~

Men of few words are the best men.

— William Shakespeare

~

Brevity is the soul of wit.

— William Shakespeare

~

Words, like fine flowers, have their colours too.

— Ernest Rhys

~

A word spoken is an arrow let fly.

— Thomas Fuller

~

The arrow belongs not to the archer when it has once left the bow; the word no longer belongs to the speaker when it has once passed his lips.

— Heinrich Heine

~

Words are under your control until you speak them; but you come under their control once you have spoken them.

— Anon.

~

In the end, we will remember not the words of our enemies, but the silence of our friends.

— Martin Luther King, Jr

~

Better than a thousand hollow words, is one word that brings peace.

— Gautama Buddha

~

It is better in prayer to have a heart without words than words without a heart.

— MK Gandhi

~

The short words are best, and the old words are the best of all.

— Winston Churchill

~

We are masters of the unsaid words, but slaves of those we let slip out.

— Winston Churchill

~

I have never developed indigestion from eating my words.

— Winston Churchill

~

Action speaks louder than words but not nearly as often.

— Mark Twain

~

All our words are but crumbs that fall down from the feast of the mind.

— Khalil Gibran

~

A picture is worth a thousand words.

— Anon.

~

Kindness in words creates confidence. Kindness in thinking creates profoundness. Kindness in giving creates love.

— Lao Tzu

~

Truthful words are not beautiful; beautiful words are not truthful. Good words are not persuasive; persuasive words are not good.

— Lao Tzu

~

A word is not the same with one writer as with another. One tears it from his guts. The other pulls it out of his overcoat pocket.

— Charles Peguy

~

Work

Working towards success will make you a master. But working towards satisfaction will make you a legend. Strive for excellence and be a legend.

— Anon.

~

Labour is man's greatest function.

— Orville Dewey

~

Work is the greatest remedy for all the problems. So work, work, work; and work faithfully.

— Anon.

~

Pleasure in the job gives perfection to the work.

— Aristotle

~